Tatta
V°

Sun

Published by Ladybird Books Ltd.
A Penguin Company
Penguin Books Ltd., 80 Strand, London WC2R 0RL
Penguin Books Australia Ltd., Camberwell, Victoria, Australia
Penguin Group (NZ), cnr Airborne and Rosedale Roads, Albany,
Auckland 1310, New Zealand

2 4 6 8 10 9 7 5 3 1

Printed in Singapore

www.ladybird.co.uk

BAMBI

Taha Siddiqui

Ladybird

It was early morning in the forest. A sleepy owl settled down to snooze in his tree, tired out after a long night's work. But his nap was soon disturbed by a great twittering and chattering, as news of a wonderful surprise spread through the forest.

"Wake up, Owl!" shouted a little rabbit called Thumper. "It's happened! The new Prince is born!"

All the animals gathered in a sunlit clearing where a mother deer lay with her new baby.

"Well, this is quite an occasion," the owl said. "You are to be congratulated."

"Yes, congratulations!" chorused the other animals.

"We have company," the doe said, tenderly nuzzling the fawn with her nose. The baby blinked his big brown eyes and pricked up his ears.

"Hello, little Prince!" the animals called.

The little Prince tried to stand to greet his visitors, pulling himself up on his long, thin legs. But he teetered and tottered and flopped right back down.

"He's kinda wobbly, isn't he?" Thumper the rabbit giggled, hopping closer to the fawn to get a better look. "Whatcha gonna call him?"

The doe looked lovingly at her baby, now snuggled at her side. "I think I'll call him Bambi," she said.

Weeks passed, and Bambi grew bigger and stronger. Each day, Bambi's mother took him to explore the forest. There were so many wonderful things to discover! Every new day was filled with surprises, and Bambi could hardly wait to see what would happen next.

One morning, Bambi met Thumper and his family. The rabbits showed Bambi so many new things.

"Those are birds," Thumper said, pointing to a flock of baby bluebirds fluttering overhead.

"Burr!" Bambi repeated.

"Say bird!" Thumper corrected, wiggling his pink nose. "Bur-duh."

"Bird!" Bambi shouted proudly. He had learnt his first word!

Then Bambi bent down to smell a patch of brightly coloured flowers.

"They're flowers," said Thumper.

"Flower," repeated Bambi, just as a furry head popped up between the plants.

Thumper rolled on the ground with laughter. "That's not a flower!" he said.

"That's all right," smiled the little skunk. "He can call me a flower if he wants to."

Bambi had made another new friend!

Suddenly, the sound of a huge clap of thunder filled the forest.

"I think I'd better go home now," Thumper called, as he scuttled back into the woods for cover. Bambi returned to his warm dry spot just as the first flash of lightning crossed the sky. He nestled close to his mother and was soon lulled to sleep by the gentle pitter-patter of rain.

The next day, Bambi's mother took him to the meadow. It was lush and green and dotted with clover and blossoms. Bambi darted out ahead, eager to run in the wide-open space – but his mother leapt in front of him.

"You must never rush out on the meadow!" she scolded. "There might be danger!"

Bambi's mother went first, moving silently and looking from side to side. When she was sure it was safe, she called for Bambi to join her.

Before long, Bambi found a shimmering pond hidden in some tall reeds. He bent his face close to the water and stared at his reflection. He saw a fawn that looked exactly like him.

But as Bambi watched, there were suddenly two reflections in the water – and one was definitely not him! It smiled and laughed and fluttered its eyelashes.

It was another baby deer – a girl – and she teased and tickled him, until Bambi nervously ran behind his mother's legs.

"That's little Faline," his mother explained. "Go on," she nudged him. "Say hello."

Bambi closed his eyes and gulped. "Hello," he said as Faline giggled.

Suddenly, Faline pounced and Bambi stumbled backwards, landing with a loud splash in the pond. Faline poked her head through the reeds and licked his face playfully. Bambi squirmed and chased after her, butting her with his head. Before long, the two were best friends.

Out in the meadow a group of stags came galloping by. Then another stag – the biggest one of all – stopped and looked straight at Bambi.

"Why was everyone still when he came on the meadow?" Bambi asked his mother.

"Everyone respects him," she whispered. "He is very brave and very wise. He is the Great Prince of the forest." He was also Bambi's father.

The silence was shattered by a loud blast. Bambi thought it sounded like a clap of thunder. But it was a gunshot – Man was in the forest.

All the animals stampeded, heading for the safety of the forest.

"Mother, where are you?" Bambi shrieked, frantically trying to find her.

"Bambi! Bambi!" he heard her cry. "Hurry!"

The Great Prince guided him to his mother and their space. Once again, they were safe from danger.

Time passed swiftly, and Bambi woke one morning to find the wind had turned cold and the whole world was covered in a soft white blanket.

"It's snow," Bambi's mother told him. "It means winter has come."

Thumper tried to teach Bambi how to skate, pushing his back legs up, then pulling his front legs straight. But they both ended up in a heap, skidding and sliding across the glittering ice.

Winter was fun at first, but after a while, Bambi longed for the warm spring days that had brought with them delicious grass and flowers.

Then one day, they found a small patch of grass pushing up through the snow in the meadow. Bambi nibbled hungrily, but noticed his mother wasn't eating. She had lifted her head to listen.

In the distance, a gun shot rang out. Bambi's eyes widened in fear. Man was in the forest again.

"Quick, run for the wood, Bambi!" his mother instructed. "Don't look back!"

Bambi ran and ran, his heart pounding as his hooves kicked up snow behind him.

"Faster!" he heard his mother call. "Keep running!"

A second shot rang out and Bambi didn't stop running until he reached the safety of his spot in the wood. Only then did he turn to look for his mother. But she was nowhere to be seen.

"Mother!" Bambi screamed into the snowy woods. "Mother, where are you?"

Bambi was crying when he sensed a tall shadow standing over him. It was the Great Prince.

"Your mother can't be with you anymore," the stag said softly. "Man has taken her away."

Bambi lowered his head sadly and swallowed back his tears.

"Come, my son," the stag told him.

Bambi looked sadly back at his home in the wood one last time. Then he followed the Great Prince into the forest.

Time flew quickly, and the long winter was at last over. Spring brought with it many changes. Bambi was now a handsome young buck with antlers, Thumper was a large rabbit, and Flower a fully grown skunk.

"Well, well – look how you've grown!" said Owl to the three friends. "It won't be long now before you're twitterpated!"

Bambi, Flower and Thumper looked at each other, puzzled.

"Nearly everybody gets twitterpated in the springtime," the owl explained. "You get weak in the knees and your head starts to whirl." The friends agreed that being twitterpated sounded awful.

But it wasn't long before Flower met a pretty skunk and fell in love with her.

Thumper was the next one to be struck by the mysterious condition Owl had warned them about. A beautiful bunny waved hello with her ear and rubbed noses with him. Thumper's foot began thumping.

Bambi still didn't quite understand what twitterpated was until he saw a familiar reflection in the water as he was drinking from the pond.

"Hello, Bambi!" said a sweet female voice. "Don't you remember me? I'm Faline." The doe giggled and licked his face.

Bambi felt suddenly dizzy, as if he were light as a feather. This, he thought, must be what Owl meant!

But someone else liked Faline, too. A young stag appeared and tried to take her away from Bambi.

The two deer locked antlers, tossing each other against the hard ground. Bambi fought fiercely, pushing the stag to the edge of a cliff. Then he butted the stag with all his might, sending him rolling down into the river below. The stag limped off into the forest, leaving Bambi and Faline alone.

From that day on, Bambi and Faline were always together. They made their home in the wood and lived happily, until one morning Bambi sensed danger in the forest.

"It's Man," the Great Prince told him. "There are many this time. We must go deep into the forest."

Fear spread among the animals as the men drew nearer.

"Bambi! Bambi!" Faline cried in terror. She could hear the sounds of angry dogs close by. She scrambled up steep slopes, just as a pack of snarling hounds burst out of the bushes behind her. Barking and biting, they chased her up a rocky cliff, snapping at her heels. She was trapped!

Just then, the dogs turned to attack something else. Bambi was fighting them off so Faline could flee! As he charged with his sharp antlers, Faline bounded up the cliff to safety.

Bambi had fought off the pack of dogs, but he couldn't escape man's rifle. A shot rang out, and Bambi fell. He raised his head weakly to see smoke pouring through the trees and animals running in fear.

Once more, his father appeared at his side. "You must get up!" said the Great Prince.

Bambi staggered to his feet and began to run. Smoke filled the air, and red flames spread over trees and bushes, surrounding the once beautiful forest in an eerie orange glow.

"Follow me," the Great Prince said. "We'll be safe in the river."

Bambi and his father leaped high in the air, disappearing down the falls just as a flaming tree crashed inches behind them.

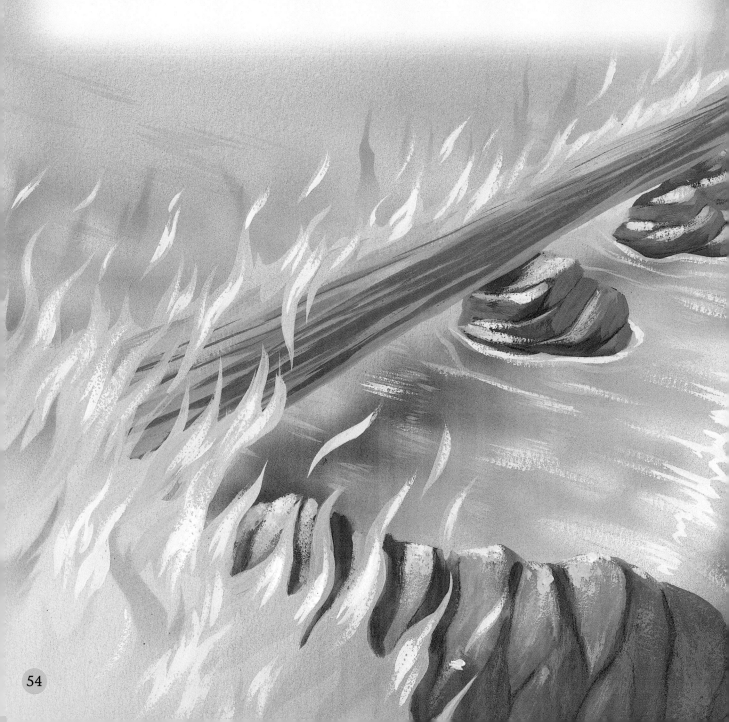

Faline was waiting for Bambi on an island in the middle of the river. She gently licked his wounded shoulder. They watched that night as fire destroyed their forest home – all the towering trees and delicate blossoms were now blackened. But tomorrow, they knew, when the fire was out and Man was gone, the animals would bravely rebuild their homes.

Before long, spring returned to the forest and the animals all gathered to welcome Faline and Bambi's new family.

"Well, sir, I don't believe I've ever seen a more likely looking pair of fawns!" the owl said, nodding his head. "Prince Bambi ought to be mighty proud."

Bambi stood with his father on a hill overlooking the spot where Faline lay with their new fawns. He was now the new Great Prince of the Forest, and he would teach his children the ways of the world that he had learned himself a long, long time ago.